D0520469

M. E. AND MORTON

M. E. AND MORTON

Sylvia Cassedy

Thomas Y. Crowell   New York

M. E. and Morton
Copyright © 1987 by Sylvia Cassedy
All rights reserved. No part of this book may be
used or reproduced in any manner whatsoever without
written permission except in the case of brief quotations
embodied in critical articles and reviews. Printed in
the United States of America. For information address
Thomas Y. Crowell Junior Books, 10 East 53rd Street,
New York, N.Y. 10022. Published simultaneously in
Canada by Fitzhenry & Whiteside Limited, Toronto.

Library of Congress Cataloging-in-Publication Data
Cassedy, Sylvia.
    M. E. and Morton.

    Summary: Eleven-year-old Mary Ella, ashamed that her
older brother Morton is a slow learner and longing for
a friend of her own, is astonished when the flamboyant
new girl on the block picks Morton for a friend.
    [1. Brothers and sisters—Fiction.   2. Learning
disabilities—Fiction.   3. Friendship—Fiction]
I. Title.   II. Title: ME and Morton.
PZ7.C268515Me 1987   [Fic]   85-48251
ISBN 0-690-04560-3
ISBN 0-690-04562-X (lib. bdg.)

Designed by Al Cetta
2 3 4 5 6 7 8 9 10

For Ned

M. E. AND MORTON

PROLOGUE

Once, back in third grade, my friend Wanda from school told me something so scary I never forgot it.

I was visiting in her beautiful bedroom on Calvin Boulevard, which is the street where all my rich school friends live, and after we had sat there for a while, not doing anything, I said, "Let's play poor children."

She stared at me. "Poor Children? I don't have it." She thought it was a board game or something.

"No," I said. "I mean, let's play we're poor. Let's play that all the stuff in this room is really junk. Let's play that we're sisters and we have no mother and father and we live here all by ourselves and we have to beg for money."

At first I had to do most of the pretending, because she didn't know how to play, but after a while she got really good at it, and the game lasted all afternoon. We played that her four-poster bed, with its pink ruffled canopy and frilly pillow, was a broken-down shack with no walls and a cardboard roof. We played that the vanity table, with its pale flowered skirt, was our school—a Gypsy tent with tattered sides and a dirt floor where we scratched out our lessons with a stick. Its cushioned bench was a mongrel at the door.

"Let's pretend that it's raining outside," I said, huddling on the bed, my hands over my head.

"No, *snowing.*" She was really getting to like this a lot. "It's snowing all the way up to the roof, and we have nothing to wear except these old rags."

"And all we have to eat is some dry bread," I said.

"That we found in a garbage pail, and it has blue mold on it," she shouted.

"And we drink snow that we collect in cups."

"No, in our *bare hands.* We don't have any cups. In our bare hands that we can't move because our fingers are frozen solid."

"And for toys we have to play with trash in the street," I said. "We make dolls out of cigarette butts."

"With candy wrappers for dresses."

"And dead grass for hair." We were both shouting by now.

"And we take them skating on those little patches of ice where people spat on the sidewalk."

"Yeah, that's where they skate. On frozen spit."

It was a lovely game.

But then her mother came in and spoiled it all. "Don't play that," she said. "That's not a nice game. Play something happy."

But it *was* happy. "Why did she say that?" I asked Wanda when her mother had left. "Why can't we play poor children?" I asked, although I thought I knew: Her mother didn't want us to play poor children because she thought *I* was poor. She thought that because I lived over on Jefferson Place, and not on Calvin Boulevard, *my* house probably had a tin roof, too, and no walls, and that when it snowed I had to huddle in the middle of the floor. She thought because I went to school on a scholarship, I probably ate moldy bread like the poor sisters in the game, and drank melted snow from my hands. She thought I wore rags to school and skated little cigarette dolls on frozen spit. She thought it wasn't polite of Wanda to play a game that was the same as my real life.

I didn't think about the dead parents part.

"Why can't we play poor?" I asked, not wanting to know.

"Because if you play something bad it will come true," she said.

"What?" I couldn't believe what I had heard.

"Yeah. Make-believe games come true. The bad ones."

"They do?" I stared at her a long time. "If you play poor you *get* poor?" I began to imagine what it would be like if all of a sudden I had to wear rags and eat moldy bread and move away from Jefferson Place. Not that Jefferson Place is so great; it isn't, really, but my apartment building is pretty nice, with a green awning over the front door and everything, and, anyway, it's where I live. What if I had to move somewhere else, to some shack without walls where the snow blew in, and the rain, too? Someplace near a tattered school with a dirt floor and a mongrel growling at the door?

"I knew somebody once who played broken leg," Wanda went on, "and she *got* a broken leg. *Two* broken legs, as a matter of fact, because she played the game twice. She was in a wheelchair for a year."

"She was?" Wheelchair was one of my favorite games. I played it in my head all the time. I'd be terribly sick in my game—gravely ill, the doctor would say—and I'd spend all my days in a padded chair with great big wheels at its sides. Each morning my mother and father would wrap a blanket around my frail legs and take turns pushing me along the sunny paths in the park. People would look at me as we went by and then look away, not wanting to stare, but one or two would stop anyway and ask, "What happened?"

My mother's answer would float over my head. "She's gravely ill," she would say, and I would repeat the words to myself, liking them, especially the "gravely" part. Gravely. It reminded me of burials and mounds of earth. Then whoever it was would turn out to be a talent scout or someone like that, and he'd make me a poster girl for some disease with initials, and my picture would be in buses and subway cars all over the city. The *country*.

I also played scarlet fever and funeral—my own funeral, where everybody came and said how nice I had been and how smart.

"Make-believe games come true?" I asked again. "Even if you don't play them out loud? Even if you just play them to yourself, in your head?"

"Yeah, it doesn't matter. It's like someone is inside you all the time, listening, and they make it come true, like a bad wish."

"A bad wish?"

"Yeah, sort of."

"How soon?" I asked in a whisper. "How soon do they come true?"

"I don't know." She was smoothing out the bed now and replacing the pillow, which meant it was time for me to go home. "Sometimes it takes a while."

*   *   *

After that, I stopped playing wheelchair and funeral and poor children. I played games where only nice things happened.

I played rich.

I played twins.

I played movie star.

I played funnies. Each day I opened the newspaper to the funny pages and picked out a comic strip with a family I liked. Then I pretended to live with them— with Blondie and Dagwood, or with Charlie Brown. I followed them around their houses, walking my fingers from frame to frame, entering their rooms, belonging to them, whispering their names. "Hello, Blondie," I'd say. "It's me—Mary Ella." And she would answer, "Oh, Mary Ella. How nice you look today, with the red highlights in your hair and all."

I played Easter egg, which was a game I made up after my Aunt Sophia came for Easter dinner one day and gave me one of those frosted plaster eggs where you can see whole scenes of rabbit families when you hold them up to your eye.

I played First Lady.

About a year after I visited Wanda in her bedroom, I asked her how come she had played poor children with me if she had known that make-believe games came true, and she just looked at me. She didn't even remember having said that.

I remembered, though, because she was right: *half* right. Make-believe games do come true, but not the bad ones, with the bad wishes. It's the *good* make-believe games that come true.

I know, because one of mine did.

But not the way you'd think.

JUNE

CHAPTER ONE

The awning goes up in front of my apartment building every March, and it's the first green of spring to appear on Jefferson Place. It isn't even real green. It's the color you get when you forget to leave a space for the sun in your painting, and you have to yellow it in right over the blue sky. Gray-green, really, but it's a color I like; and each year, although I have seen it appear many times, it takes me by surprise. I turn the corner on my way home from school one day and there it is—a long shell of canvas stretching like a giant caterpillar from the doorway of my building to the curb.

All winter long, my street—with its vacant awning frame, its bare trees and hedges, its empty fire escapes, its blank sidewalks—looks like an unfilled page in a coloring book: all hollow spaces and dark lines. Now, though, suddenly, the first of those outlined spaces has been colored in. The awning frame, naked as a skeleton from September until March, is spread with lovely green, and I hold my books against my chest—hug them, really—as I contemplate it from the corner.

Later, little by little, more green comes to color the open spaces on Jefferson Place. Slender stripes of moss fill in, as though with a careful crayon, the narrow bands between the paving blocks, and black-green leaves, so brittle they snap in two when you fold them in half, sprout among the tangles of the hedge across the street. Soon, pots of spiky plants appear between the railings of the fire escapes, and three weeks or so after the awning goes up, the framework of branches on the maple at the corner is spread with a gray-green awning of its own. But it is that first stretch of green, that sudden bloom of canvas on the frame above my door, that lets me know for certain spring has come.

The awning itself doesn't really provide much protection from anything, as awnings should. It's full of holes, for one thing, so it's no use in the rain, and it offers no shelter from the snow either, because it isn't up when there *is* snow. But we always gather under it anyway, just as cats collect under a car, because it seems like a safe place to be.

Also, the awning tells the name of my house. "275 Coolidge Court 275," it says, in gray-white letters along its hem. All the apartment buildings on Jefferson Place have names, although none of the others has an awning, and all the names except one are those of presidents. Van Buren Arms. Monroe Court. Polk Terrace. (The only way I knew that Polk had been a president was that his name is woven into the doormat of the apartment house next door, and once, when my teacher asked who Henry Ward Beecher was, I raised my hand immediately and said he was a president, too. But Beecher Mansions, it turned out, is the one building on Jefferson Place that is named after somebody else.)

Another good thing about my awning has nothing to do with the green canvas part, but with the metal legs that support its frame at the curb: two upside-down V's, slender and strong and perfect for turning somersaults on. Every now and then someone will leave a game on the pavement, go over to those bars, and turn a somersault, quick as those toy bears that flip, feet over head, when you squeeze the two wooden rods at their sides.

I was turning a somersault myself, or trying to, the day Polly first appeared on Jefferson Place, and that is why, in my earliest memory of her, her face is upside down. It was the second week in June, and my school had already closed for the summer. No one else's had, though, so I was all alone on the block, and I was feeling good. I like it when everyone is in school and I have the street to myself. Also, I was wearing shorts outside for the first time all year—purple nylon shorts with those built-in underpants that are really designed for boys—and I liked the feel of elastic tight around my thighs and of the air moving up and down my legs. And the privet hedge across the street had just begun to bloom. Everywhere among the leaves were fuzzy flowers, pale as soda foam, that smell of beginning summer, of new shorts, of heat, of games in the street. I love that smell.

I was gripping the awning bars hard and leaning far, far back, practising my somersault, with the top of my head about to touch the ground, when I suddenly found myself gazing upside down into the face of a girl I had never seen before. The odd thing was that for a moment her face didn't look upside down at all. A pink Band-Aid taped across her forehead looked to me like a grim smile in the center of a broad chin, and her hair—a tangle of loops like those script ℓ's I scribble around the faces of my drawings—became, from that angle, a frizzy beard. She looked, in fact, like one of those trick pictures where you see either a bald man with lots of whiskers or a curly-haired child, depending on which way you hold them up.

The fact is, I really couldn't turn a somersault at all, although I practised a lot when no one was around. So, as soon as I realized I was being watched, I held still and pretended instead to be examining some exciting event on the underside of the awning, like a circus acrobat or something. Anyway, I gazed carefully upward for a long time, hanging on to the awning bars and scraping the ends of my hair against the sidewalk. I especially wanted this new girl, whoever she might be, to notice my long hair, which somebody once said had red highlights and which somebody else once said was my one nice feature.

I wanted her to notice a lot of things about me. The way I laced my sneakers, for instance, so that the bow was at the bottom of the row of holes instead of at the top, and the way my necklace shone like real gold. I had been tieing my sneakers upside down for four months, hoping somebody would notice them, but nobody ever did, and nobody ever noticed my necklace either, with its one hundred and fifty-four S's linked, tail to tail, into a chain so fine I could coil it into the letters of my name.

Every night, when I was alone in my room, I would pretend that someone was watching me from my window and admiring all those nice things about me. That was how I played Easter egg, the game I began when Aunt Sophia gave me that egg with the scene inside. In my game, I lived in one of those eggs and some strange girl peered at me through the glass. "Oh, hey," she'd say, "look how she ties her sneakers!" Or, "Look at that necklace with all those golden S's." Just the day before, I had sewn my initials in little red cross-stitches on all my T-shirts, and the girl at my egg window had noticed them and said nice things.

Now I wanted this new girl to notice them, too, and to wonder about them. "How come it says 'ME' on her T-shirt?" I wanted her to say to herself. I wanted her to wonder, too, why I was out on the street at a time when everyone else was in school, and to guess finally that I was home not because I was sick or cutting classes, but because I went to a private school that closed for the summer earlier than everybody else's.

Most of all, I wanted her to notice that I lived in Coolidge Court, the only building on the block with its own awning, the only one with furniture in the lobby and metal blinds on all the windows instead of paper shades. The best house on the block. Mine. I wanted her to notice that, and to wish that she were me.

It was nice hanging there, letting my hair fall to the ground, feeling the eyes of this new girl linger on my red highlights, on the chain at my neck, on my embroidered letters, on my sneaker laces, on *me*—the one who went to private school and lived in the only building on the block with an awning.

I hung there so long that when I finally straightened out, I felt dizzy. The privet hedge across the way drifted out of focus, and a storm of silver fireflies took flight before my eyes. It was a while before I could turn to meet her eyes, but when at last I did, I found that the sidewalk was empty, and the new girl who was to have been my audience had, in fact, moved on and wasn't there at all.

CHAPTER TWO

I didn't see her again until the following week. I was under the awning that time, too, but not practising somersaults. Instead, I was sitting on the curb, making sunrays with a Popsicle stick out of a puddle in the street. Doing nothing, really. Everyone was still in school and the afternoon was quiet. Suddenly, though, there came a clicking sound, and I looked up to see her, the new girl, on the opposite sidewalk, running a piece of chalk against the iron pickets that surrounded the privet. She walked quickly, leaving behind her, like a message spurted out by a skywriting plane, an even row of soft, pale dashes.

A Band-Aid was still spread like a grin across her forehead, but the tangled loops of her hair were bundled now behind her head with a piece of string—the kind you tie up packages with—and this time she was wearing lipstick. *Purple* lipstick that went outside the lines at the corners of her mouth. I watched her secretly, with my chin on my knees, as she progressed along the street.

When she reached the end of the iron pickets, she paused in front of the privet and searched for something among its leaves. For what? I wondered. For anything, it could have been; things always get caught in the tangles of that hedge—nice things, some of them: jack balls, for instance, that have escaped from some wild throw, and squares of colored cellophane that turn the sky to fire when you hold them to your eye. Feathers, too—gray, usually, but sometimes blue— to smooth between your fingertips; and money, even— Henry found a dollar bill there once, folded neatly like a soft green moth among the twigs.

She could have been looking for any of these things, but, as it happened, what she wanted was a leaf. She plucked one off carefully, and I waited for her to do with it what I always do with privet leaves—fold it in half and listen to it snap. Instead, she curled it up and put it in her mouth.

Hey, I wanted to call out, *don't eat that! It'll make you sick!* I knew, because I had once tried eating a privet leaf myself, choosing one that was crisp and shiny as vinyl and curling it over, just as she had done, before sinking my teeth into it. It hadn't really made me sick, but it had been bitter, and I had spat on the sidewalk a long time afterward, trying to rinse the taste from my tongue. *Don't!* I wanted to cry, but by then she had picked off another and was eating that one, too. Anyway, I wouldn't have called out to her at all. I didn't even want her to know I was watching.

I looked at her secretly, though, for a long time. First I watched her eat the leaves, and then I inspected her clothes. They were not like what anybody else I knew ever wore. Her skirt, for one thing, came far below her knees, and it seemed to be about fifty years old. It was made of wide bands of black, yellow, and red, and it looked like those costumes we wear year after year in school plays—those of us who don't get good parts and end up being peasants. She wore it with a plaid flannel shirt that was too big on her and, anyway, was too warm for a day in June. Together they made her look like—what? An outsider, sort of, like someone from someplace far away, and I wondered suddenly why *she* wasn't in school in the middle of June.

Maybe she was foreign, I thought. Maybe she had just come from someplace where everybody wore long skirts and ate privet leaves. Maybe she needed someone who could teach her things and show her around. A guide. Maybe *I* could be her guide. I could teach her new words in English. "This is a gold chain," I could tell her, hooking my thumb under my necklace and showing her its tiny gold S's. "Say 'chain.' No, *'chain.'* That's better. Now say 'gold.' "

Next I would point up to the awning. "Look," I would say. "Awning. Say it: 'Awn. Ing,' " and I would show her other green things on Jefferson Place: green moss, green plants, green leaves, green privet. I would show her the initials on my shirt and my upside-down shoelaces and my pretty hair. I would pick off a flower from the hedge and hold it under her nose so that she could sniff its beginning-of-summer smell. "Flower," I would say, and not laugh when her tongue tripped over the *l* and the *w*. Later, after it was clear that I was her friend, I would take her around to everyone else on the block. "This is Gemma," I would say to them, showing her off. "I'm teaching her to speak English. Hey, Gemma, what's this?" and she would answer, "Gold chain," making it sound funny.

She had turned around now and was running the chalk against the pickets with her other hand. Just as she reached the point opposite me, she stopped and sat down in front of the fence, tucking her long skirt under her knees and staring in my direction. I instantly returned to the wet, flat sun on the asphalt at my feet, and moved my Popsicle stick like a paintbrush across its surface. The puddle was coated with oil, and it held in its center a swirl of colors that shimmered like the throat of a pigeon as I pulled at it this way and that, around and around.

Maybe, I thought next, she had run away from home and hadn't had anything to eat in a long time. Maybe she was hiding in the old abandoned shed at the end of the block, emerging only when she thought no one else was around and picking privet leaves from the hedge. It would be nice, I thought, to have a secret friend who lived in a shed. I could take things to her every day—little things that nobody would miss: pieces of meat put aside from my own dinner, and a stem of grapes folded into a napkin. Old clothes, too: shorts and T-shirts for now, and, in the winter, last year's mittens, if I could find them, and my old coat.

I stretched each sunray into a skinnier and skinnier point, connecting their tips into a spoked wheel. If I leaned far enough forward, I could see my face melt into its hub like a blurred photograph, and I stared at it a long time, watching my eyes swim about like quiet fish. How did people start talking to each other anyway, I wondered, even if they both spoke English? What did the first one *say*? I hadn't made any new friends in a long time; everyone I knew was either from the block, where they'd lived as long as I could remember, or from school, where I'd known them since first grade.

[24]

Pretty soon the public-school kids would come home, and one of them—Deirdre, most likely—would spot the new girl and know immediately what to say, and the new girl, even if she knew no English, would smile, and they would go off together. After a while, they would come up to me, hand in hand, and Deirdre would say, "This is Gemma. I'm teaching her English. Say 'awning,' Gemma." That's the way things always end up with me.

The pink end of the Popsicle stick had turned black in the water, and the other end, pale as cream a few moments ago, was becoming gray in my hand. The new girl began to rub her chalk against the sidewalk, drawing something, and once she looked up at me, but I didn't return her glance. She probably wasn't foreign at all, I decided. Lots of people wore clothes that didn't match, and lots of people ate crazy things—pencil erasers, for instance, and paper reinforcements, and those dried bits of skin that grow around your thumb. Privet leaves were no crazier to eat than thumbnail skin, when you stopped to think about it. And she probably wasn't a runaway, either. Nobody would run away *to* Jefferson Place. Still, it would be nice to have a new friend, especially before anybody else had a chance to get to her.

Soon, I told myself, my sun puddle would dry up, and when it did I would walk across the street and say something. What? *Do you like privet leaves? Do you want this Popsicle stick? Is your name Gemma?* What could I say? *What's that you're drawing?* That might be good. *Can I see your picture?* Something like that. I would rehearse it first so it came out just right. Then, by the time Deirdre and everybody else arrived, the new girl would belong to me. We would sit side by side under the privet, playing hangman on the sidewalk with her chalk, and after a while we would walk under the green awning together, and go into my lobby with all the nice furniture and up to my apartment with the metal blinds on the windows, and she would be my friend. "Let's see your picture," I practised into the puddle.

But the puddle didn't dry up at all, and we sat there a long time, I with the oily sun at my feet, she with the chalk drawing at hers. Every so often a car would pass between us and cut off my view of her, the way a head in front of a movie projector suddenly darkens the screen, but the rest of the time I could sneak looks at her whenever I wanted. Now and then she would look at me and then return to her chalk, making quick, long strokes on the sidewalk, shading them in with the side of her fist, tilting her head to inspect what